The Circus Is Back...

M.D. LABELLE

This is for those of you who have always feared clowns or circuses and have no clue why.

Titles of some of M.D. LaBelle's other works to look for:

The Circus

The Bad Behavior Series

The Soul Eater

The Lake Series

Cursed Blood

Casper's First Halloween

The Luna's Mate: The Alpha King

The Lusting After Mr. Knight Series

A Birthday For Momo

My Nightmares

Sophia

Chapter 1: The Night Before Halloween

It's now the night before Halloween in the small town of Coupeville where a fog creeps in slowly and the Circus begins to arrive on a strange cool breeze. As they roll unexpectedly into town, they all feel this immense sense of excitement. For they know all too well that some little boy or girl will soon be their next meal.

Not a living soul notices as the tents magically pop up out of nowhere as if they are ghosts in the night. Eerie music plays softly as the Ringmaster's minions smell innocence in the air from the town just beyond their gates. So of course, when one of them dressed in all white with frills and caked black paint around its eyes catches a whiff in the air particularly appetizing, it gathers a few of the others before they make their way to the outskirts of town.

Just as soon as they reach a small blue house with a white picket fence, the tallest of them begins to sing a mesmerizing melody of which is barely a whisper. As they stand there looking monstrous in the moonlight with their gaping jaws wide open and their eyes all aglow like a blazing fire, the front door begins to move inward. Within a few seconds, a starry eyed 6-year-old named Cindy Smith pokes her head out at first and then slowly creeps into the night.

She cautiously glances around in front of her before hesitating and turning to make sure no one is coming after her before she shuts the door. However, when she hears one of them accidentally kick a stone across the street, she freezes in place for a moment because she is unsure of what to do next. After scanning the darkness, she spots the small group of misfit clowns and immediately the fine hairs on her arms stand on end.

Seeing that they are about to miss their opportunity, they all start to sing louder, and the music begins to take control of her legs again. She walks forward unwillingly while she fights every step and wishes that she had just stayed in bed. Suddenly she tries to cry out, but she quickly realizes that there is no point when nothing comes out of her mouth.

No more than a moment later, tears begin to cascade down her little rosy cheeks, as she whimpers silently into the darkness. The clowns begin to circle around her, salivating and grinding their teeth hungrily. They close in on her tightly before a monstrous claw picks her up and the clown carries her back to the circus rolled up under its arm without anyone else knowing. Once there, it drops her to the ground with a loud echoing thud in front of the ringmaster's tent as they all begin to growl angrily and hunch down like wild animals about to fight over a small piece of their prey.

It is at this exact moment that little curly-haired, pale-faced Cindy, frozen with fear, decides to close her eyes and pray like her mom taught her just the day before. The closest one with huge eyes that bulge from its sockets, notices this and starts to laugh demonically before leaning down to say, "God can't hear you now little one, and even if he did, he wouldn't care anyway."

Afterwords, she watches as it opens its mouth wider than it should be able to before its sharp teeth sink into her sweet meat. All the while, it stares hatefully at its meal with soulless black orbs. She winces and then tears flood her eyes as her flesh rips. Finally, she is allowed to cry out, but this only serves to make them all frenzy.

Among the sounds of her pleading frantically and her screams, they tear into her and shred her chest open. One of them spreads her ribs with its claws and you hear a loud snapping sound, then it scoops out her heart before holding it up to the moon. It shrieks and then gobbles it up while still warm like the monster that it is with bright red blood dripping down its face, slippery wet and a Cheshire cat smile from ear to ear.

One only knows the sheer pain she went through as they opened her while she was still alive, but as the white of her bones glistens in the night, her lifeless body already starts to grow cold. Within a mere matter of minutes, her body is torn from limb to limb as her blood sprays all over their faces and her head detaches from her neck with a loud pop. The crunching of bones and tearing of ligaments echoes within the ringmaster's tent before he opens his door and walks out.

"I do believe that you didn't wait for me at dinner. How rude! I have told you time and time again that I want to be present when you find such delicious morsels. Now, let me through to take my turn." The ringmaster exclaims as he pushes one aside violently before swiping Cindy's discarded left arm from the ground.

He picks it up and holds it before his mouth as he takes a big bite out of it, then he tears the skin clean off the bone. Now, I can only imagine that if an outsider were to see this, it would probably remind them of a turkey leg at Thanksgiving dinner.

"Mm. I do declare that this is one of the best meals we have had in quite a while. After all, older children's flesh is just not as sweet as those that are still so innocent." he murmurs under his breath and then a long, thin forked tongue licks the blood clean off his lips.

"You know what to do when you are done making a mess. Do make sure that there is absolutely no trace left of her because we don't need problems like we had before." he reminds them as he walks back to his tent to prepare for tomorrow.

After all, tomorrow is the big day, the one and only show because they realized that sticking around for more than one day lends to questions that don't need to be answered. However, before he steps back inside, he turns around briefly as he burps up a small piece of her bloody skin loudly and then swallows it back down again. When he does, he watches as the last bit of Cindy Smith's blood is slurped up off the ground and one of the demons disappears with her shredded clothing.

He can only assume that they will start their bonfire with it tonight before dancing in the moonlight without their human skins on. What he doesn't know is that this demon has been keeping souvenirs of their kills. Something that may catch up with them later if anyone starts looking into more disappearances.

A few hours later, as Cindy's mother and father get up for their busy day, they find that her bed is cold, and the covers have been thrown off as if she hurried to get out of bed. Immediately, they call Sheriff Charlie Summerton, who then calls in his deputy Tony Carleson to investigate. However, when they are forced to bring in the dogs, they turn up nothing and end up going home empty handed a few hours later.

Chapter 2: There Is Always That

"I am hungry Vlad." A short and extremely fat demon with baby legs whines pathetically as it rubs its belly slowly with a frown on its grotesque face.

"I can't believe you ate without me. I told you that I would be back, but you didn't wait for me and now my stomach is growling louder than ever. Please….please…? Do you think I could just snack on one infant before the acts get started? I will be careful as can be to make sure that no one sees me." It pleads as the ringmaster glances at it with disdain on his face.

"No, now go away. I warned you not to leave because the others were going to get food, but you made the choice not to listen. You will just have to wait until it is time. Now, go." The ringmaster shouts while pointing with his long and black bony finger towards the rising sun.

However, as he stares at the fat demon and then at the sunlight hitting the tents, he thinks of a better idea for him. While watching everything turn from old to shiny and new with the first light of day, he decides what to say.

"On second thought, perhaps you could do something for me." The ringmaster states softly just before his eyeballs begin to slide out of the sockets and swing gently in the morning breeze.

The demon nods quickly before hearing exactly what he has up his sleeve.

"Put on your costume and then head into town with this." the ringmaster adds as he unrolls a worn paper flyer with The Rondell Family Circus on it.

As he looks down at it one last time before handing it off, he checks to make sure that it reads 4 p.m. on Halloween and then rolls it back up. Once he leans down and the overweight demon wraps his claws around it, he returns to his tent to put his own human suit on again. For very soon someone will take notice of the Ferris wheel or the sounds of the elephants as they echo through the woods towards the town.

On the way back, it stares at all the cages as the animals turn into living and breathing things instead of piles of old bones.

"Hello Sam." It stops to say before reaching his hand through the cage and rubbing the old tiger's ear as it leans into his palm.

"Just another town, another night and then we will be gone again." The clown murmurs under its breath before hurrying onward.

Soon enough, it makes its way back to the sleeping quarters before it slips on its clown outfit and smiles creepily with murderous intent.

"Oh, how I would love to sink my teeth into a baby finger right now and suck the flesh right off the bone." It murmurs quietly and then pictures a baby in front of it.

Suddenly, it remembers what the ringmaster said, so it hunches over and sighs because it knows all too well that if it doesn't do what he says, it will pay for it later when darkness falls upon this little town. After turning around to face the mirror, it quickly plasters white paint on its face and finally resembles a clown before smirking one last time with delight and then walking to the town square.

Upon entering the main part of town, it sees an old wooden electric pole with posters stapled to it, so it smiles and then adds this one over top of the others. Afterwards, with a quick flick of its wrist, it turns around and watches as a mother casually walks by pushing a stroller with a red-haired baby inside.

"Mm. How convenient and so tasty." It thinks to itself before looking around to make sure that no will see it following her.

As it scans the area one more time, it cautiously follows behind her for several blocks, while hanging clear back. Eventually, when she starts to walk down a dark alley in a less populated part of town, it rushes to catch up. Without making a noise, it runs up behind her and extends its long, sharp thumbnail so it can slice the woman's jugular.

Quickly she stops in her tracks as if she senses it, so the clown is forced to strike before it is fully ready. With one precise motion it slits her open from ear to ear. No more than a second later, a bright red jet of blood sprays across the clown's face as she fights for air, and she tries to scream. However, there is nothing but the sound of gurgling from the gaping slit in her neck.

She clutches her throat as if doing so will stop the air from escaping the wound, but it only helps for a second or two before she collapses into a pile of her own warm blood on the ground. When her eyes become hazy and lifeless, the clown begins to giggle in delight. That is precisely when it hears the baby wake up and start to cry.

"Hush little one. Don't worry. It will all be over just as soon as I find some place where I can eat you without prying eyes." It whispers next to the baby's head as its long scaly tongue licks the baby's ear slowly from top to bottom.

"So sweet. I almost can't wait to eat you." It whispers again before pushing the stroller quickly to an even darker corner where no one can hear the baby's cries but the clown.

A second later, there is a bone crunching sound that sends shivers of excitement down the clowns' spine as it bites one of the baby's fingers clean off and then pops it in its mouth like a French fry. Then it slips the skin right off the bone as it makes a sucking sound before grinding it to powder. All the while, the baby girl begins to scream in pain as the clown stares at it hungrily and blood seeps all over the pale-yellow baby blanket in her stroller.

"Oh, little one. Make as much noise as you can." It yells at the top of its lungs before it cries in unison with the baby loudly.

But when the clown grows even hungrier, it stops and stares at the little one for a second or two before leaning in and wrapping its long sharp nails around her thin little neck. Another quick pop and then the sounds make their way to the clowns' ears as its belly growls.

"Now to quickly eat and get rid of the evidence before anyone sees me." the clown murmurs under its breath.

As its mouth slowly opens into an abnormally large gaping hole, it scoops the limp baby up in its arms carefully because the blood makes it slippery to hold. Then it slowly but surely sucks in the baby's whole head in first. When it reaches the broken neck, it makes a choking sound as it struggles to get past the shoulders, then you hear tendons snap, ligaments pop and bones breaking as the mouth stretches even further to take in the rest of the baby's body. Like a snake that is eating its prey.

Once the clown successfully swallows the baby's body down into its stomach to digest, it pushes the stroller over to the dumpster behind an abandoned warehouse and rushes back to the Circus without anyone ever noticing it.

Chapter 3: The Sheriff

"I am about to go out there now." 25-year-old Deputy Carleson replies after Sheriff Summerton who is 11 years his senior, asks him to go check out the Circus.

No more than half an hour earlier, Mr. Danvers, a 52-year-old widower with grey hair, called in to the station because his dog was growling and acting very strangely upon approaching the gate at the fairgrounds. He had admitted to himself that it just didn't sit right with him either as they strolled all the way around the fenced in area while Jonny, his 8-year-old beagle, barked loudly. Then as soon as his Jonny was done going to the bathroom, they high tailed it back to his house so he could notify them right away.

"Well, just make sure you keep a sharp eye out and call me right away if there is any trouble." Sheriff Summerton warns because his gut tells him that there is just something off about this one, but he has to file the paperwork on the disappearance of Cindy Smith before he can join him.

"Not only did Cindy just go missing, but then the circus shows up out of nowhere in the middle of the night and at Halloween of all times." He thinks to himself while remembering something from his past.

Sheriff Summerton has always hated circuses and clowns ever since he was little when his father left with them and never came back. He had often wondered if that was his plan all along or if some other forces were at play that night. Either way, if he could help it, he would rather not make a trip out to the circus today or any other.

"Cassie, I know you are really enjoying that sucker but why don't you come over here and lick this instead?" he says snidely as he tries his best to forget about the circus.

For a second, he thinks that she may take him up on it because she turns around and bends over in front of him slowly while her blonde hair cascades down over her 28-year-old voluptuous curves. But when she continues to suck on the candy instead of him, he realizes that she is just antagonizing him and feels the anger start to boil over within him.

"O.K. then." He murmurs under his breath before watching her stand up and smirk.

Quickly, he raises his fingers to her throat and wraps them around it then he slams her body against the wall with his. The first thing he notices as his fingers squeeze, is that her skin feels so soft while his lips claim hers. When she returns the kiss, he releases her neck and steps backwards.

"You needed to be punished because you are getting too cocky." He explains while his hand immediately goes to his zipper to straighten himself before anyone else sees.

"Awe. But I liked it. I think that after you get that paperwork filed, we should keep going." She replies in a sexy voice while batting her eyelashes at him flirtatiously.

"God, you are going to be the death of me girl."

As soon as he sighs and shakes his head, she runs her manicured pink fingernails over his zipper and ends at his belt. She smiles sweetly before she reaches up and kisses him on the lips. Just a quick peck but boy does it get him hard as a rock.

"You really know how to get me going. You know that right?"

"Mhm…." She answers softly before walking away and sitting down at her desk.

A few seconds later when the phone rings, she picks it up and answers quickly, "Hello, this is the Coupeville Sheriff Department. How can I help you?"

"Alright. Let me check." She says as she looks at the computer in front of her and starts to type on the keyboard.

"I guess this is my cue to get on that paperwork." he says quietly as he shuffles his feet towards his desk.

He has always despised doing paperwork, but he knows the longer he waits, the less chance they have of actually finding little Cindy alive.

"If only someone would just find her wandering around." He murmurs as he stares at the white pages in front of him.

After he fills out the forms and sends them to the other towns surrounding Coupeville, the fax machine suddenly begins to whir and spit out copies upon copies. He stands there for several minutes as it continues to spit them out. Eventually, when it has completed its task and only one piece of paper remains, he takes them off the machine. He glances over the pictures before stopping dead in his tracks after reading the information under one of them.

"Ann Taylor, age 5, was reported missing two years ago after a small family circus came to town. They investigated but came up with nothing and there has been no trace of her since then." He reads aloud softly as he skims through the file.

While sitting down and shaking his head, he begins to wonder if this circus is one and the same.

"Cassie. Can you do me a favor?"

"Let me guess. You want me to give you head?" she replies playfully right before her phone rings again.

"No. I mean I wouldn't mind, but right now is not the time. We may have a problem on our hands. I need you to contact Tony and make sure everything is alright while I call Sweetwater." He explains as he looks in his desk for the sheet with the other towns' phone numbers on them.

"Why, what's up?" she instantly asks while cocking her head because curiosity has gotten the better of her.

"No time. I am hoping I am not right." He says worriedly as he looks over the papers on his desk again.

"Go, go call him." he demands as he raises his voice.

She instantly runs to her desk before calling Deputy Carleson with concern in her voice, "Tony. Have you made it out there yet?"

"Yeah, it looks fine to me. As far as I can tell, it is just a plain old run of the mill circus. I can even hear the elephants. Other than that, I think we are going to have to wait until closer to the show this afternoon because the gates are locked, and no one seems to be around to let me in." he says breathlessly as he walks back to his car and puts his hand on the hood.

"Alright. Thanks. Why don't you head on back then and we can have a talk when you get here. I want your two cents on something." Sheriff Summerton says as he takes the phone from Cassie and then sits down in the chair in front of her desk.

She stares at him while he hands her the phone before she finally asks thoughtfully, "Do you think Cindy's disappearance has something to do with the circus coming to town then?"

He pauses as he thinks it over and then replies slowly, "Yes. I do. However, I can't prove anything, and I think I need to contact someone that knows a little more about this than I do. But until then, I am going to keep a wary eye on that circus and the town's children."

Chapter 4: Let's Just Wait And See

A few minutes later when Deputy Carleson walks in, he glances at Cassie's messed up hair and smeared candy red lipstick before rolling his eyes. He already knows what happened.

"They were at it again." He thinks to himself as he sits down in his chair and starts to relax for the moment.

"So, you didn't see anyone inside?" Sheriff Summerton asks as an afterthought while arranging a pile of papers on his desk into rows.

They were not there when he left, so he can only guess that they came through on the fax machine while he was out investigating at the fairgrounds.

"No. Not a single soul except for the animals. It's as if they all disappeared into thin air." Deputy Carleson replies nonchalantly while putting his feet on top of his desk.

Sheriff Summerton glares at him and then suddenly asks snidely, "Do you mind?"

As soon as he says it, Deputy Carleson quickly lowers his feet and sits up in his swivel chair. When he remembers to open the bottom drawer of his desk, he pulls out a brown paper bag with his lunch in it so he can put it in the refrigerator. Then he stands and stretches before turning towards the sheriff.

"Excuse me, please. I was in such a hurry this morning that I forgot to put my lunch away in the fridge. I will be right back and then you can tell me what is really going on." He states with a furrowed brow before walking past and into the other room.

After he returns, he looks at the two of them expectantly as he waits patiently for someone to explain everything.

When Sheriff Summerton raises his voice, he announces swiftly, "There is a connection between the circus and the disappearances. I found a Sheriff on the East Coast that has been looking into this since last year. Apparently, when the circus came to his town, very bad things happened but they could never pin it on the people in the circus. That isn't even the worst part of it. When he started to investigate it further, he found that there have been disappearances for at least a hundred years all around the country. Ironically enough, the only thing that they all have in common is a circus that comes at Halloween. Every year it appears in a different town, never to retrace its steps."

He pauses and then adds, "To be honest, this sounds more like a ghost story than anything but there are police reports that back it all up."

Deputy Carleson quickly glances between the sheriff and Cassie as he begins to wonder if he is in a dream and still in bed. Deciding against just pinching himself, he sits back in his chair but listens for any more information before he asks sarcastically, "So, let me get this straight. I am to believe that someone in this circus has been killing all around the country for over a hundred years. How is that even possible?"

"Well….." the sheriff says before pausing as if he is lost in thought.

Before continuing he swallows hard and rubs the already forming stubble on his jaw.

"Maybe we are not dealing with one person. Just hear me out here. What if this circus is a family of killers and it goes from generation to generation? I do know that down in Texas they had that famous case they made that slasher film from. Damn it. For the life of me I can't remember what it was called."

Sheriff Summerton stops and closes his eyes as if he is trying to remember. No more than a minute later, he looks wide eyed at them and states jokingly, "It could be a case of cannibalism. If it was something like that it would be possible to pass it from generation to generation."

Cassie murmurs under her breath, "That is nasty. Who could do something like that?"

When silence falls upon the room, the sheriff walks over to the door and looks out the window. He stares at a few pedestrians as they slowly walk past and wonders if he should be doing more to protect his little town. But what?

"If I was absolutely certain that they were behind all the disappearances, I could shut it down before they even opened for business. However, there is no proof and that just sucks." He says as he runs his fingers through his thick black hair and silently curses their very existence.

He adds with a sigh, "Man, sometimes I wish that I didn't have to follow the rules, but we are here to enforce them. Just do me a favor and keep an eye out today, but if you hear or see anything out of the ordinary let me know right away. I am just itching for an excuse to run them out of town before anyone else decides to disappear without a trace."

"Sure. Do you want me to hang around in that part of town. I could just park the car by the entrance so I can watch if anyone comes in or out." The deputy states as an afterthought while unholstering his gun and checking to make sure the barrel is empty.

As he waits for an answer from the sheriff, he quickly disassembles it and lays out the pieces on his desk before he looks up at him in anticipation and then down again to clean and reassemble it.

"That might just work." Sheriff Summerton announces as he walks over to his desk and takes a seat before picking up the phone.

"First, I need to call that sheriff and find out if it is the same circus or not. Then, if it is, we have something to go on. Otherwise, we won't have a leg to stand on if I do end up running them out of town."

Just as soon as he dials the number, Sheriff Langley picks up and asks, "Yes? May I help you?"

Chapter 5: The History Of It

"Well…this is Sheriff Summerton out here in Coupeville. I had received several faxes from your office and wondered if we could talk."

While fidgeting in his seat, he patiently awaits his answer.

"I do have a few minutes. Why? What's up?" Sheriff Langley asks hesitantly as if he seems unsure if he even wants to get involved.

"As I told your office before, we now have a circus at our fairgrounds that very mysteriously popped up in the middle of the night. Of course, as it just so happens, we also have a missing little girl who disappeared into thin air. What do you make of it? Does it sound remotely like what you went through last year?" Sheriff Summerton says as he rifles through the papers on his desk slowly.

"It is quite possible. I would need to know more information first, but you wouldn't happen to know the name of the circus, would you?"

"Hold on. Let me ask my deputy. He is the one who went out there to check it all out." Sheriff Summerton states before pausing and switching his attention to Deputy Carleson before asking him, "Did you find out what the name of the circus is by chance?"

Quickly Deputy Carleson smiles and nods before answering, "There is a poster on the gate of the fairgrounds that said The Rondell Family Circus Come One Come All for one show only at 4 p.m. on Halloween."

"Thank you, Tony." Sheriff Summerton replies before hearing a loud sigh from the phone.

"I am assuming you heard that by the sigh." He adds as he continues to rifle through the papers until he settles on one and holds it up to his eye level.

"Yes, I did. If that is indeed the name of the circus, then it is the very same one. I would watch my back if I were you and your townsfolk because if anything happens there like it did here, I can guarantee that you won't be prepared for what is about to unfold." Sheriff Langley replies worriedly before the silence returns.

"As I recall from reading the details, there were a few disappearances, a suicide, a murder, and several unusual occurrences between all Hallow's eve and Halloween. Does this sound familiar?"

"Yes, unfortunately that is absolutely correct. We had our share of misfortunate events during the time that the circus visited us. While I could never pin it on them, I always knew that it had everything to do with them…..There is just something unnatural about the way that circus came in to town and then left so suddenly. Not to mention, when I talked with the ringmaster, he made the hair on the back of my neck stand on end. That never has happened before." Sheriff Langley states eerily.

"Interesting. Well, I hope that soon enough I will come face to face with the ringmaster myself to have a talk. Maybe then I will get down to the truth of the matter before anymore unfortunate incidents happen in our small town." Sheriff Summerton says quietly over the phone so only Sheriff Langley can hear it because the last thing he wants to do is cause a panic.

"If you really need me, I could take the next plane there, just so you have back up." Sheriff Langley states quickly as if he has somewhere he needs to be.

"No. No. I think we will be fine. I do have a deputy that is plenty handy when it comes to these sorts of things, and we will just keep an eye on them for now." Sheriff Summerton replies while reading the paper in front of him intently.

"Alright, but just remember from what I could find they have been around since the early 1800s and while I'm not a superstitious man, I know when things are not exactly what they may seem."

"Thank you. I greatly appreciate all the information and the help, but I think we can handle it from here on out. I will let you know if we have any other problems." Sheriff Summerton says shortly because he looks at the clock on the wall and realizes that it is almost noon.

"Sounds good to me. Just let me know." Sheriff Langley says sadly before ending the call.

After putting the phone down, Sheriff Summerton reads the paper over one more time. "Nothing. Not even a trace of blood. It's as if they never existed." he murmurs under his breath before shaking his head and looking up to realize that both Cassie and Deputy Carleson are staring at him.

"I just don't get it. How can so many people go missing without a trace?"

"Human trafficking?" Deputy Carleson asks quickly before laughing nervously and glancing at Cassie.

"No, I don't think it's that. Then again, I'm not entirely too sure what it is." Sheriff Summerton replies as he stands up and gets ready to head out.

Before he leaves, he glances at Deputy Carleson and adds, "Make sure you end up over at the fairgrounds before 1 and stay there. I will catch up with you when I am done, but in the meantime watch for any movement. They should be showing themselves soon enough."

"Alright boss. Just as soon as I eat my lunch, I will leave. Oh, that reminds me. On my way back Tina Hutchinson flagged me down and told me that her animals are all acting crazy as if they are scared or something. I told her I would investigate it later. On your way to the fairgrounds can you stop by her place to see what she is talking about?"

"Of course. See you then." Sheriff Summerton says quickly before sighing and walking out the old wooden door with his hand in his coat pocket.

There is something he needs to check on before he heads on over to Tina's place because his gut is telling him that Cindy Smith didn't just go missing. What he doesn't know is that someone else already has. Eventually, when Lucy Castle is reported missing along with her baby, no one will care besides her husband Phil because everyone else will already be enjoying themselves at the circus with their families.

Chapter 6: Preparation Time

"What are you all doing?" the ringmaster yells at the top of his lungs angrily as he watches a demon teeter comically on a ladder nearly 8 feet off the ground.

"Master, we were just trying to put up the finishing touches. A few of the ropes had worn through so we tied on new ones and were just about to tighten them up. Why? Does it not look good to you?" the short little demon asks hesitantly with a crooked grin and two short arms that can barely reach the banner in the first place.

"I merely ask because anyone can see you and you still have not put on your human suits. Have you forgotten where your heads are?" the ringmaster asks with concern in his voice because there are only a few hours before they open the gate.

"I am so sorry. I didn't think and of course you are right. How could I forget?" The demon quickly slides down the ladder as it straddles it between its pencil thin, grey appendages.

"My mistake. I won't do it again." He adds before rushing off to his tent as soon as possible.

Shaking his head angrily, the ringmaster murmurs under his breath, "What would they all do without me? I wonder sometimes."

He then quickly removes the ladder before anyone gets any more smart ideas and places it behind the lion's cage.

"How are you doing today my dear?" he asks the lion sweetly as he reaches between the bars and begins to stroke the lion's mane softly.

"There, there. Soon enough the show will start and then we will have our fun. Won't we my sweet? I promise this time that you can grab a small child if you want." He whispers sweetly as he continues to pet its soft fur and it closes its eyes.

"Now, I must go and make sure that they aren't doing anything foolish for the humans to see. Sometimes, I just wish that I didn't have to watch over them all the time." He says softly before sighing and retrieving his hand.

When the lion realizes that he has stopped petting him, he roars loudly but then the ringmaster yells, "Now, that is quite enough. If you want to have a sweet treat, you must behave. Now, hush!"

No more than a second later, he scowls and then leaves angrily. Afterwards, he continues to walk around the small circus to make sure that everything is in order for their opening. But when he sees that half of the demons are not dressed and in makeup, he growls and screams at the top of his lungs, "What do you think you are doing? Have we forgotten that we cannot be seen as we truly are? You would think after all these years that you would get your heads out of your asses! Now, before I count to ten, I demand that all of you go to your tents and slip into your costumes before I send you back. Do you so easily forget that I can make you disappear just as easily as we do them? Now go before I decide to get rid of all of you."

With those words, they quickly rush back to their tents. One by one they carefully slide on their suits before applying the paint to their faces to hide their true selves from prying eyes.

"One of these times I will replace him as ringmaster." a rather large demon murmurs under his breath as he paints two black circles around his eyes, and then puts contacts in so they don't see the big black orbs that peer back at them.

"I just know that I would do so much better than him. After all, he is getting old, and I am three hundred years younger." He remarks carelessly until he realizes that Vlad is standing in the tent's doorway.

"Oh, really. Just because you are younger does not necessarily mean better. I have so many more years of experience and am far more mature than you will ever be." He barks before he smirks with devilish intent in his eyes.

With a flick of the ringmaster's finger, the demon goes up in flames right before him as the smell of sulfur fills the air.

"One less minion to watch over when there are plenty more to take your place. Good riddance." He murmurs before leaving the tent.

When another demon watches him leave the tent, he asks, "What happened?"

"Don't you worry. Just clean that mess up and then you will have a tent to yourself." The ringmaster suggests before the demon smiles from ear to ear creepily and quickly walks inside.

On the way back to his tent, the ringmaster notices something. There is a sheriff's car parked by the locked gate with a man inside. He seems to be watching for something.

"Well, let's go say hi and make a new friend." The ringmaster says sarcastically before walking over to the gate and unlocking it.

He smirks and then with a big push the gate opens with a loud squeak. It is enough to cause the Deputy to turn his head and stare at it. He watches as the ringmaster walk towards him slowly, then suddenly the deputy opens his door. The ringmaster stops in place before saying pleasantly, "Good afternoon. I am sorry that I didn't see you sitting there sooner but I have been busy getting everything ready for our show."

As the ringmaster watches the deputy fake a smile and then climb out of his vehicle, a cold wind blows that seems to chill him, then the deputy notices goosebumps form on his exposed flesh. The ringmaster already knows that the deputy will have tons of questions that he has no time to answer right now. After all, it is only two hours before the gates open for business, and the ringmaster still needs to make sure that everything is ready. It's just a good thing that he didn't come half an hour earlier or he would have disappeared like all the rest.

"Well, good afternoon to you too." Deputy Carleson says to the extremely tall, thin man in front of him as he thinks to himself how much he looks like a character straight out of a horror movie.

Chapter 7: Something Is Just Not Right

The moment Deputy Carleson steps inside the gates, he knows something is up because all the circus clowns start to stare at him as if he is their next meal. As they walk by, he even catches one of them whispering something eerily to another clown without even caring if he heard them or not, "Why can't we just kill him and get it over with. No one will know."

When the ringmaster hears them whispering, he gives them a warning glare and clears his throat before stating, "Excuse them, they are pranksters but are completely harmless, I assure you of it. After all, how many times have you heard of a clown hurting anyone?"

"And I assure you that I am not scared easily. Besides, I am here because there has been a disappearance, and it is ironic that just as a little girl disappears your circus rolls into town." Deputy Carleson replies before adding, "Say, by chance have you seen a five-year-old girl walking around the fairgrounds? Or anything out of the ordinary?"

"Well, I don't know what you consider out of the ordinary, but I will keep an eye out for the little girl." The ringmaster comments and then holds his huge hand out to gesture for the Deputy to lead the way.

As Deputy Carleson begins to walk ahead, he notices that he gets this uneasy feeling in his gut as if there is something terribly wrong, but he can't put his finger on it. So, he carefully pays attention to his surroundings and watches all their movements. Unfortunately, nothing immediately sticks out as overly off so once they are done walking around the circus he is forced to leave them to their own devices for the moment.

He turns around once they are at the gates and states thoughtfully, "I shall leave you now and hopefully I will get a chance to see the performance when it is time."

"No problem officer, we are more than happy to have you. Now, as you can see, I still have things to take care of before our opening. Thank you for stopping by."

With that in mind, Deputy Carleson quickly walks back to his car. The whole time the hairs on the back of his neck are standing on end and his arms are covered in goosebumps. For some reason, while he was inside those gates, he felt as if the temperature had dropped 20 degrees or more and he was scared for his life. Never had he ever felt this way before. Never.

There is just something wrong with that circus. Whether it be the strangely odd misfit clowns, or the way that the ringmaster always sounded just a little bit off and mildly sinister. It just made his visit feel like he was standing in a den of vipers.

Once he sits down and pulls out of the parking lot, he runs his fingers through his dark brown hair before radioing it in. "Deputy Carleson here. I was just out at the fairgrounds when I saw movement inside. I watched them for a few minutes before the gates opened and the ringmaster appeared. Boy, when I tell you this man is creepy, it is an understatement. He is abnormally tall and lanky. Every time he talked, there was this underlying evil intent to his words or his voice. I can't decide which one, but either way I felt threatened as if they just wanted to make me disappear along with the others. Now, I am coming back to the station to file a report because I really don't think it is necessary to keep watching them when it opens in less than two hours."

"Sure, enough then. We will see you when you get back. Thanks for giving us the heads up." Cassie says flatly as if she is doing something else more important.

Deputy Carleson shakes his head and laughs because he wishes that just once she would be doing him. After all, she is the prettiest thing in Coupeville, and he has had a sweet spot for her ever since he moved there two years ago after getting the job. She was the first friendly face he saw when he moved to town and ever since then he has hoped she would see him for the man he really is.

Before he says too much, he hits the radio button and continues to drive.

"God, what I wouldn't do for her." He murmurs under his breath as he pulls in the parking lot.

Upon returning to the office, he opens the door and realizes that Sheriff Summerton is not back yet.

"He is still not back?" Deputy Carleson asks Cassie after sitting in his chair and drinking a mouthful of really bad cold coffee.

"Nope. He mentioned something about he had to go do something and then he would have a talk with Tina Hutchinson about her animals. But I haven't heard anything from him since he left. Do you suppose I had better reach out to him?"

"Hm. I would just in case he ran into any problems." Deputy Carleson replies hesitantly as he works the sore muscle on the back of his neck with his fingertips.

As she picks up the radio, a thought pops in his head. "I wonder if he ever made it to Tina's?"

"This is Cassie here. Pick up Sheriff Summerton if you can."

There is a moment of silence and then when he doesn't say a word, she finally clicks the button off.

"So, what do you think he is up to? I know that Cindy Smith's parents have been calling all day. I feel so bad, but we have nothing to tell them." Cassie asks as she straightens out her skintight black top that shows far too much of her cleavage.

"Well, hopefully he is over at Tina's and is finding out what is causing her animals to act strangely. I have a hunch that it has to do with the circus because of all the animals and the weird sounds. I doubt that her animals are used to that." Deputy Carleson replies softly while subconsciously staring at her breasts.

"Can you not do that?" Cassie asks hesitantly as she lowers her eyes and then looks away at the door.

"What?"

"Stare at me as if I am a piece of meat. I am a person not just a walking vagina" she says hurtfully before standing up and walking out of the room.

"Stop. I am sorry." He yells as he stands up quickly and runs after her.

When he finds her in the kitchen, she is crying softly over the coffee pot. He grabs her by the forearm and turns her around before he sees the teary eyes and the red face. Instantly, he feels ashamed for what he did and cups her cheek before asking sweetly, "Can you please forgive me? I am really sorry. I just had a momentary lapse of judgement, and while I know that is no excuse, the fact that you are so beautiful sometimes makes it hard to think of anything else."

She quickly turns away from him and then replies in a whisper, "I know. I guess I am just having a bad day and with that little girl missing it is just making it worse. I don't mean to take it out on you though. Can we just forget I ever said anything?"

After a few seconds of silence, Deputy Carleson answers quietly, "Yes."

Realizing that she needs her space, he walks out of the kitchen with his shoulders hunched and feeling bad about what he did.

"Where is everyone?" Sheriff Summerton asks as he walks in the door and sees that no one is sitting at their desks.

Chapter 8: Answers

"Yes?" Deputy Carleson replies worriedly when he sees Sheriff Summerton's face.

"I just came back from Tina's place, and she is right. Her animals are acting very suspiciously. Not even her old goat will go near the river by the fairgrounds. It's as if they know something we don't. I checked around her property for any signs of hazards but didn't find a single thing. So, now I am back to the circus and if it has anything to do with it." Sheriff Summerton states slowly while watching Cassie walk back into the room.

He could already tell that she had been crying and the guilty look on Deputy Carleson's face can mean only one thing. However, he has no time for this now because he is the sheriff, and he has people who need him regardless of how he may or may not feel about Cassie.

"Tony, can you do me a favor and go back out to the fairgrounds. It is almost time for everyone to start arriving for the show and I want you to make sure that everyone stays safe. I will be out there shortly, but I need to make a phone call first."

"Alright. But did you ever figure out what you were going to before?" Deputy Carleson asks curiously as he looks between the two of them.

"Yes, I stopped out at the Smith's and asked them a couple of questions. They didn't know anything but at least I was able to cross them off the list for possible suspects. Now, of course we are no closer to finding her, but then again, I don't need to go looking in their closet for her dead body either."

"Good to know." Deputy Carleson replies sadly before opening the door and walking out.

When Sheriff Summerton sits down at his desk and picks up the phone, he dials Sheriff Langley's number before waiting for him to pick up.

"Hello, this is Sheriff Summerton again. I am really sorry to bother you, but I need to ask you something. Did you notice anything odd about how the animals acted around the circus? We have a farmer that lives next to the fairgrounds and all her animals won't go to the watering hole because it borders with it."

"Now that you mention it, I do remember when the circus came to town all the dogs started to bark simultaneously before suddenly stopping. The whole time it was in town, the animals did stay away from it too. Do you think it has something to do with it?" Sheriff Langley asks hesitantly before adding, "Did you ever get to meet Vlad the ringmaster. He is something else alright."

"No. However, my deputy did. I didn't get to talk to him about his encounter with the ringmaster, but I gather it was relatively uneventful or he would have had plenty to tell me when we saw each other briefly."

"Well, speaking of that I really should get going. I am supposed to meet him out there before everyone else arrives for the show." Sheriff Summerton states quickly after sighing.

"Be careful." Sheriff Langley murmurs before ending the call.

After he takes a few quick bites of lunch, Sheriff Summerton heads out to the fairgrounds without ever talking to Cassie about what happened. However, on the way, the radio beeps and then he hears Cassie's voice as she tells him that Phil Castle has just filed a police report for the disappearance of his wife Lucy and their baby. Apparently, she had gone out for a walk with the stroller while he was going to work. This afternoon when he came home, he looked for her everywhere and could not find her.

"Thanks, Cassie, for letting me know. I am almost at the fairgrounds now. As soon as I get there, I will let Tony know and then we will double check the fairgrounds first before canvassing the town. Over and out."

When he sees the parking lot, there are families starting to line up and the lot is almost full of cars. He can already tell that almost everyone from Coupeville is here and just hopes that nothing bad happens while everyone is inside. A few minutes later, as he drives by the front, he sees Deputy Carleson's car, but he is not inside.

"Tony, now where did you go?" he asks himself while looking from side to side in search of him.

Stopping the car finally, he gets out and sees Deputy Carleson standing next to the entrance. He is talking to an extremely tall man wearing brightly colored clothes. Sheriff Summerton automatically assumes he must be the ringmaster before he even walks up to talk to him.

"Ah, yes. You must be Vlad the ringmaster. Am I correct?" Sheriff Summerton asks loudly while everyone watches.

"Why, yes. And you must be Sheriff Summerton. Your good deputy here has filled me in on your name already. I am glad to meet you and I do hope you will come inside to see the show today." the ringmaster says politely before a sinister grin begins to spread across his lips.

"Say, we seem to be missing a mother and her baby now too. You wouldn't have seen a woman walking with a stroller by chance?" Sheriff Summerton asks carefully while watching for the ringmaster's reaction.

Before the ringmaster answers the question, he places a cold outstretched hand onto Sheriff Summerton's shoulder and then calmly states, "No, I honestly can say that I have not seen anyone out here before the two of you and the crowd started to show up. The parking lot and the grounds have been empty since we arrived."

"Alright, thank you for your honesty. We must leave for a bit but will be back because I do want to see the show. I am most curious of what is involved."

"But of course, I look forward to your return." The ringmaster replies before turning his back to them and walking to the front of the line slowly.

"Now, shall we." He announces loudly so everyone can hear, and the line begins to move to the ticket booth while everyone takes their turns paying for their entrance fee.

Deputy Carleson turns to the sheriff and asks quietly, "Now who is missing?"

Sheriff Summerton whispers, "Lucy Castle and her baby. Phil came in this afternoon and filed a police report while I was on the way out here and Cassie had just contacted me before I arrived. I told her that we would check out the grounds before heading into town."

"Oh, damn. That can't be a coincidence."

"Nope, my gut tells me that the circus and that ringmaster have everything to do with it, but I can't prove anything just yet."

Once they walk outside of the circus grounds, they head to town. When they arrive, it feels eerily like a ghost town because everyone is at the circus except for Mr. Henley who is locking up his barbershop and Mrs. Tanner the mail lady. She is far too busy with packages to go to the circus.

"Well, I guess there is nothing else we can do right now but to go back to the circus and keep an eye out. After all, he has already filed the police report and after everyone goes home from the circus, we can organize a search party for Cindy and now Lucy with her baby." Sheriff Summerton states sadly after they searched high and low throughout the town for Lucy and the baby.

Chapter 9: The Show Has Started

After they return to the fairgrounds, they park their cars and Sheriff Summerton looks around one last time at the completely full parking lot before he heads in. He can already hear the cries, ooohs and ahs of the people as they watch the show before he even gets the chance to watch it for himself.

"I see you are certainly enjoying yourself." Sheriff Summerton states snidely towards Deputy Carleson as he watches the elephants parade in front of everyone around the circle.

Sheriff Summerton can't help but get this awful feeling that something bad is about to happen. So, when he sees the clowns leave with the elephants and the crowd goes wild with excitement, his hand instantly goes to his side where his holster is. But when he sees the woman in tight black leather riding a motorcycle high above them in a ball, he temporarily relaxes. Surely, nothing bad can happen right now. So, he decides to sit down in a row towards the back where he can still see everything going on. Deputy Carleson takes a seat by the front just in case there are any problems.

"You should be aware boys and girls that she is riding with no restraints. So, if she makes a wrong move, she will fall to her death. Keep watching for the ride of destiny as the flames consume her and she overcomes all odds." the ringmaster announces over the loudspeaker clearly with everyone's eyes on the ball.

Suddenly, we hear a loud crack before fire shoots out, then the ball becomes filled with flame and surely there is no way she can get out. The crowd starts to scream when they realize she has been burned alive. However, no more than a few seconds later, everyone hears the motor roar through the smoke, and they see the lights of the motorcycle flashing against the top of the big tent.

The crowd roars when the smoke clears, and the fires die down so everyone can see her riding around in the ball. When it starts to slowly descend, they clap, and the joyous roars of the crowd grow louder yet. Of course, when the ball touches the ground, the door opens, and she rides out miraculously unharmed.

"It is amazing boys and girls. She looks as if there was no fire at all. Now come one come all as we bring in the King of the Jungle. The lions." He yells as the motorcycle disappears out the back of the tent and the lions rush in while roaring.

With teeth glistening in the bright lights, the regal lions take their perches before the ringmaster walks onto the stage with a red and white candy stripe oversized hoop. He smiles at the crowd while wearing a bright red suit jacket and white parachute pants. When he walks over to one of the lions he whispers in its ear, "Now it is time my sweet.

Remember at the end of your show, you can pick whichever one you desire."

Once again, the lions roar on cue and then all eyes are on the ringmaster as the hoop instantly is aglow with flames that burn brightly around it. He holds it out to the side of him before he whistles and the smaller lion leaps forward through it unharmed. The second, larger lion jumps through with just barely enough room, but it is also unharmed.

After returning to their stands, they begin to roar again loudly before the ringmaster turns around and smiles. He winks at Deputy Carleson right before the biggest lion leaps off its pedestal and into the crowd. Too late, the deputy pulls his gun as the lion takes Jimmy Perkin's head into its mouth and clamps down. The crowd screams as they begin to run out of the tent and pushes him down.

Jimmy's parents stand there shocked as they watch the lion shake its head violently before blood sprays everywhere. When it does, his head makes a popping sound. The lion bites down harder as it rips clean off the vertebrae and more bright red blood sprays everywhere. The crowd screams even louder as they run out of the big tent for fear of their own lives while Mr. and Mrs. Perkins stand there helpless looking on.

Mrs. Perkins, not even caring that the lion is still standing there, drops to her knees and cradles her lifeless son, blood and all while Mr. Perkins cries out before rushing the lion. Unfortunately, for him, the smaller lion decides to join and latches onto his shoulder with its sharp canines. It refuses to let go as searing pain shoots throughout his arm. He screams at the top of his lungs as the lion rips his arm clean off. Blood spurts all over the row as he grabs the place where his arm was. However, he soon finds that now there is just gristle and cartilage protruding from where the bone was.

Briefly Mrs. Perkins takes her eyes off her son to see why her husband is screaming. When she realizes what has happened, the lion attacks him again and his blood sprays her in the face before she faints.

As Sheriff Summerton sees all of this helplessly from the back, he tries to move forward as they all push him closer and closer to the exit. "Stop! You must let me through!" he demands as he yells loudly to no avail.

Everyone is so scared that they are just trampling anyone in their way. Finally, when almost everyone is out, Sheriff Summerton rushes towards the stage area where the victims are, and Deputy Carleson is trying to control things the best he can. He watches as Deputy Carleson rips off the bottom of his shirt and cries out, "Call for an ambulance as he does his best to control the bleeding, even though it is far too late for that now. It is obvious that Mr. Perkins has lost too much blood because he is lying on the ground barely moving.

As for Mrs. Perkins, she is still unconscious, and no one would want her to wake up to this scene in the first place. So, as the scene enfolds, Sheriff Summerton rushes over to Deputy Carleson's side and yells over the lions' roars from the back of the tent, "Go outside and flag the ambulance down. I will stay here to make sure they are safe from harm. Now go."

Without ever thinking twice, Deputy Carleson picks up his weapon and runs outside. He waits for the ambulance who arrives within a matter of minutes and then guides it inside. Once Mr. and Mrs. Perkins have been carted off to the hospital, the coroner arrives, and within an hour or two they take little Jonny to the morgue.

The smell of heavy metal still lingers in the air as Sheriff Summerton and Deputy Carleson make sure that the lions are of no harm to anyone else while they watch the clowns put them back in their cages and lock them up tightly.

Chapter 10: Cleaning Up The Mess

Just as soon as they talk with the ringmaster, animal control comes out and they put the lions down quickly without an incident.

"Do you suppose this all could have been avoided?" Deputy Carleson asks Sheriff Summerton as they leave the tent less than an hour later.

"Probably not. But then again, we still have three missing persons cases to solve so does it really matter now?"

Deputy Carleson shakes his head in disgust when he realizes that Sheriff Summerton is right.

"With everything going on I managed to forget about that. How can three people go missing in one 24-hour period from a town that never has any problems? That is the mystery." Deputy Carleson says quietly while trying to figure out what has happened.

"Should we keep looking around? It will be dark within an hour and a half and then we won't be able to find anything. Not to mention, these clowns are creepy, but I don't see any of them carrying out a murder and making them completely disappear without a trace." He wonders as they watch the last of the cars leave.

"No, why don't you just go back and see if you can talk to Phil. While you are at it go to his house because there may be something that can possibly lead to where she is. For all we know she could have left him and didn't leave a note." Sheriff Summerton replies quickly as he scans the area for anything that may help them find the missing citizens.

"Fine, but what if we don't find them? Then what? After all, that is an awful lot of people to go missing."

"Look. All we can do is try. I haven't seen any indication that they have anything in common so at least a serial killer is out of the question." Sheriff Summerton replies quietly as the breeze grows colder towards the evening and they walk to Deputy Carleson's squad car.

As soon as Deputy Carleson opens his door, Cassie's voice can be heard on the radio, "Pick up. We have a visitor, and he wants to speak with you Sheriff Summerton. He says it is important and I think you are going to want to meet him."

"Hold on a minute. Who is it?" Sheriff Summerton asks as he picks up his own radio.
"Why, it is Sheriff Langley himself. Apparently, he hopped the first plane here so he can chat with the ringmaster of the circus." Cassie replies as she stares at Sheriff Langley.

"Yes, that is exactly right. I did." Sheriff Langley interrupts as he takes the radio from Cassie and then adds, "Are you out there at the fairgrounds right now?" Sheriff Langley asks quickly.

Sheriff Summerton hesitates before answering, "Yes. We are. Two of the lions attacked the crowd so we had to clean up the mess here. Between the ambulances, the coroner, and animal control, we have had our hands full."

"What did you just say?" Sheriff Langley asks while sounding extremely concerned.

"Two of the circus's lions attacked the crowd. In the end, one little boy died, the father lost his arm and the mother fainted because she couldn't take it. The doctors think she has lost her mind because when she woke up all she could do was scream and no matter what they did they couldn't get her to calm down. I just guess it was all too much for her to see her child and husband being torn to shreds.

The worst part was that little Jimmy's head popped as it was torn clean off right in front of her." Deputy Carleson states softly as he remembers every grizzly detail.

"I feel so bad because I had my gun pointed at the lion, but I couldn't get a clear shot and then I was trampled." he adds as Sheriff Summerton pats his back.

"Well, look. Since you are already out there, I am going to take the taxi and meet you. I do believe Cassie said it is only about 10 minutes away, correct?" Sheriff Langley asks quickly because he is afraid that the circus will disappear again before he gets to confront them.

"Yes, yes, it is. We will meet you here then. I look forward to it." Sheriff Summerton replies before the radio goes dead.

"Alright then. I guess we will hang around here for a few minutes. Shall we take one last look around before he arrives?" he asks thoughtfully before walking towards the gate.

Fortunately, they hadn't locked the gate yet, so Sheriff Summerton takes the time to walk inside, and he starts looking around. Deputy Carleson catches up and asks quietly, "What do you hope to find that we didn't see before?"

Sheriff Summerton shrugs his shoulders before whispering carefully, "I was hoping that they would mess up and we would find something to help us locate the others."

"So, why are we slinking around here?" they hear a familiar voice ask from behind them loudly as they turn around and see a tall man in his mid-forties walk up to them.

He instantly takes a hold of Sheriff Summerton's hand and shakes it excitedly before he smiles at Deputy Carleson.

"I don't suppose you all would know where I can find the ringmaster would you? I have a bone to pick with him or three and I have to do it quickly before they go and disappear on me again." He states quickly as he looks over the tent in front of them.

Seeing that they are the only ones in the near vicinity, Sheriff Summerton replies curiously, "Nope. Can't say that I do. I haven't seen anyone for a bit. Now that you mention it, I haven't even heard any of the elephants."

"That is not good. That means they are preparing to leave, and I have no time. Well, let's see if we can find the ringmaster then, shall we?" Sheriff Langley starts to walk towards a sound from the opposite side of the tent and towards the front but then suddenly stops dead in his tracks.

Chapter 11: Evil Always Wins

"Hello there. I don't recall seeing you here earlier. Why, this is not your town so why are you here?" the ringmaster asks snidely as he glares down at Sheriff Langley.

"Oh, so the two of you have met before." Sheriff Summerton interrupts quickly before Sheriff Langley ever gets to say anything.

"Excuse me, but yes, we have. If you remember right, I told you all about it earlier. If you don't mind, I need to have a private word with Vlad here because we have some catching up to do." Sheriff Langley announces as he steps towards Vlad and glares menacingly at him.

"I know what you did and have done so many times before. Now, what I don't know is how you did it, but I am pretty sure that you are not exactly human. Are you?" Sheriff Langley accuses as he leans in too close to

Vlad's face and he spots something there that scares him, pure evil.

"To be honest, I don't have a clue what you are referring to. I am as human as you are. As for those little boys and girls that went missing, I have a hunch that you will find them years down the road. But it is no matter to me whether you find them or not because I have not done anything wrong. Now why don't you take your armed thugs and get the hell out before I have to file charges for harassment!" the ringmaster says in a whisper while practically spitting in Sheriff Langley's face.

"Maybe we had better leave." Deputy Carleson admits while wrapping his fingers around Sheriff Langley's forearm.

Sheriff Summerton begins to move forward to block just in case there are problems, but he is all too late when suddenly Sheriff Langley punches the ringmaster in the face with his right fist.

The real problem is that the moment his fist connects with the ringmaster's cheek, it should have done something. But instead, his fist sort of slid across the ringmaster's face like he was hitting Jello. It bounced and then made a squishing sound before he realized what had happened.

As soon as his brain registers what happened, he hits him again with twice as much force. This time he punches him in the nose and instead of a squishing sound, a loud crunch is heard. Sheriff Langley watches as a large amount of dark red blood sprays from the ringmaster's nose and lands on Deputy Carleson's Sheriff jacket. In the meantime, the ringmaster just stands there with a shit eating grin on his face as if he is rather enjoying it.

"Stop, Sheriff Langley. This was just not called for." Sheriff Summerton announces as Deputy Carleson quickly wipes the blood off his jacket the best as he can before they grab Sheriff Langley by both arms and slam him up against the electric post with a loud thud.

"If I had known what you were about to do, I would have never let you come out here. After all, despite what you feel, you know damn well that we are here to uphold the law, not to break it. You have no jurisdiction here. Therefore, this is totally uncalled for." Sheriff Summerton states authoritatively before he glances at the ringmaster and asks quickly, "Do you want to press charges?"

"Yes. Yes, I do. I don't believe that an officer of your stature should act as you have. As the other Sheriff said, you are hired to uphold the law, not to break it." The ringmaster says eerily while running a hand over his cheek and squishing the misplaced tissue back into place. For some reason, no one notices except for Sheriff Langley who just looks on in disgust.

"Fine. You are under arrest for harassment and assault. If you wish to be represented by an attorney......" Sheriff Summerton says as he speaks only a few sentences of his Miranda rights before they take him back to the car.

On the way out, Sheriff Summerton looks back at the ringmaster and states loudly, "I will be back so you can sign some official paperwork when we have him secured safely in the vehicle."

"What was that about?" Sheriff Langley whispers to Sheriff Summerton when he thinks this is just for show.

"What was what about? You really are being charged and are going to be thrown in jail because we can't have vigilantes running around, now can we. You stepped over a fine line and now he will get away scot-free all because you couldn't wait until they messed up."

"But you know that they will leave before that happens. They always do and then no one will see or hear from them until next year when more kids disappear to never be found." Sheriff Langley states sadly because he knows it is already too late.

He had his chance and fucked it up good. That is unless….

"Deputy Carleson, stay here with him while I take a formal complaint." Sheriff Summerton demands as he turns around to walk back to the gate.

Upon arrival, he watches as the clowns scurry around taking banners down and locking all the animals cages in preparation for their departure.

"Will you be leaving today?" he asks the ringmaster thoughtfully as he looks up at him and wonders how he doesn't look like he was punched in the face twice just a few minutes earlier.

"We hadn't planned on it but given the circumstances we may very well. I haven't decided yet. Besides, we are preparing now for an after party so the clowns can have some fun before we must leave again. It is my way of giving back to them because of all the hard work they put into it." The ringmaster replies absentmindedly as he seems to be thinking of something else and stares off towards the town.

"Well, I do need to take the formal complaint so we can file the paperwork when I get back to the office. The courts like it all neat and dotted on the lines." Sheriff Summerton states quickly when the ringmaster starts to walk towards the nearest tent without paying any attention to him.

"Yes, yes. Where do you need me to sign? It is getting late, and the sun is about to go down so you must hurry because I don't like to be out after dark." the ringmaster asks as he rolls his eyes and waits for Sheriff Summerton to pull the paperwork out of his jacket pocket.

"Here it is. I will type it up when I get back to the station, but I do need you to sign right here first." Sheriff Summerton quickly hands it to him with a pen.

The ringmaster walks over to the nearest tree and leans the paper up against it before jotting down his signature. When he hands it back to the sheriff, he asks, "Why did you not sign your last name?"

The ringmaster looks down at him with an eerie smile before replying coldly, "Because I do not have one."

Sheriff Summerton stares at him oddly for a second because he has no response for that and then quickly writes down the complaint before announcing, "This is what I wrote and what will be officially typed up when I return. "On October 31st, Sheriff Langley assaulted Vladimir on the fairgrounds. Both I, Sheriff Summerton, and Deputy Carleson witnessed the assault and harassment that occurred before we were able to apprehend Sheriff Langley and secure him in the vehicle."

"It sounds good to me. Now, will you please leave us to our own devices so we can get things tidied up. As you can see, we have a lot to do and now very little time to do it in. Thank you for all your help." He says mockingly before he adds, "I do hope they find those missing people. It is just a shame because it happens far too much."

Before Sheriff Summerton can even reply, the ringmaster has slipped into the big tent and has left him to wonder if he is really being sincere or not and why he would bring it up unless it was to rub it in their faces. After all, they can't prove anything, but the writing is all over the walls.

Chapter 12: I Guess We Have To Let Him Go Then

On the way back to the station, Sheriff Summerton stares out the window as he recalls the look on the ringmaster's face while practically bragging about the missing persons. "Damn it!"

Deputy Carleson turns briefly to glance at him before returning to stare at the road and asks worriedly, "Is everything alright?"

"No, but I wish it was. We shouldn't have had to do this, but you, just had to do this didn't you!" Sheriff Summerton yells at Sheriff Langley before returning to stare out the window angrily.

"I am sorry but if I had told you what I planned on doing, you would never have let me see him in the first place. I had to do this, but even that didn't go as planned. I tell you. That man is just not human!" Sheriff Langley replies sadly as he sits forward and tries to reason with them.

"You must let me go now so I can finish the job!" Sheriff Langley pleads with them as he closes his eyes and hopes they listen to reason.

"Honestly, I would like nothing better for you to prove that he has done something illegal but quite frankly we can't." Deputy Carleson interrupts as he drives into the parking lot of the station and shuts off the car.

After Sheriff Summerton climbs out of the squad car, he opens the back door and pulls Sheriff Langley out before whispering in his ear suspiciously, "Do you get the feeling that there will be another disappearance tonight?"

"With the way he was acting, I would say most definitely." Sheriff Langley says softly so no one else can hear.

"I was afraid of that. Deputy Carleson, after we get him booked and, in his cell, do you mind swinging back by the fairgrounds and taking one last look? Maybe, even hang around for a couple of hours to make sure there are no more problems." Sheriff Summerton adds as an afterthought before he opens the station door and walks Sheriff Langley inside.

***

Once they fingerprint him and then lock his cell with Sheriff Langley inside, Cassie rushes in and takes ahold of Sheriff Summerton's hand before pulling him out of the room. As soon as they are out of ear shot, she states quietly, "We have to let him go Charlie. Sadly, to say, you did not usher his complete Miranda rights so that makes him a free man. Judge Whittaker said that we can't hold him because it was an unlawful arrest."

"Shit! I was so caught up in everything that I didn't finish it. Well, if I let him out now, he will go right back there and cause more problems for himself. What if I just held him over night?"

"No, Charlie, you know you can't. Judge Whittaker will have your badge for that regardless of the situation." Sadly, Cassie says before she runs her fingers up his arm, and she stands up on her tip toes to kiss him on the lips hungrily.

"Just let him go. Maybe, we can have some fun while Tony is out at the fairgrounds." She suggests as her fingers run down his chest, to his belly and then to the growing member in his pants.

"Oh, hey Tony." Cassie says loudly and turns around when Deputy Carleson opens the jail door unexpectedly.

"Judge Whittaker said we have to let him go because the two of you failed to read him the complete Miranda rights." She reiterates as she stands in front of Sheriff Summerton, so Tony doesn't notice the Sheriff's erection.

"Damn. I guess we were just so busy trying to get him out of there before he got into any more trouble. Oh well. Now what?"

"I want to hold him but at the risk of losing our jobs, I guess we have no choice. I just know that he will be right back out there causing trouble." Sheriff Langley states sadly as he watches Cassie stroll to her desk and sit down.

"Well, you did say for me to go back out and keep an eye on things for several hours. I guess that means I take my dinner out there and stake it out." He says before smirking and then he asks Cassie sweetly, "Do you think you can call Jenny's and have her make me a plate up with her world-famous lasagna on it to go and a mug of hot coffee?"

"Of course. I will do that right now. Are you going to be picking it up before you go or swinging back for it later."

"Oh, if she can put a rush order on, I will get it on the way. Thanks." He says happily before he throws one of his prize-winning smiles at her.

"Alright. I will call it in right now."

"Make sure that you always keep your eyes on the fairgrounds because I just have a bad feeling about tonight." Sheriff Summerton states before he walks back to let Sheriff Langley go.

"I will give you a head start though." He adds as he quickly turns around before opening the door to the jail.

With that in mind, Deputy Carleson walks to his car before he feels this strange darkness surround him as if a bad storm is coming. So, he hurries to Jenny's Diner and picks up his order before he drives to the fairgrounds. When he arrives, he swings by the gate before parking and notices that it is already padlocked to keep intruders out.

By now the sun is setting and the moon is slowly rising overhead as he sits back to eat his dinner. He keeps an eye out for any strange happenings as he enjoys his lasagna and pours a nice cup of piping hot coffee. What he doesn't realize though is that while he is out enjoying his own meal, inside they are already preparing for their festivities which includes baby back ribs and toddler tartare.

Chapter 13: Party Time

As Deputy Carleson sits outside in his car, Sheriff Summerton slowly hands back Sheriff Langley's gun before warning him, "Don't do it. I beg of you. The last thing I want to do tonight is place you under arrest again."

Sheriff Langley laughs and then replies sarcastically, "No worries. I intend on steering clear of them. Besides, they are probably gone anyways because they tend to disappear at the first hint of trouble with the law."

When he walks out the front door, Sheriff Summerton can already tell that he is flat out lying. But then again, what can he really do if the man is hell bent on doing something?

"Honestly, do you think he will leave it alone?" Cassie asks curiously as she too fully intends on leaving for the evening.

"No. I can tell you right now that he will be back here in no time unless he gets himself killed first. But try to have a good night either way."

"Sure thing." She replies as she smiles knowingly before walking to her car and then driving out of the parking lot.

Sheriff Summerton sits down in his chair for the last time this evening as he feels thankful that at least Deputy Carleson will have a little time to himself before Sheriff Langley will have a chance to walk there. Unfortunately, what neither one of them could possibly have known is that Sheriff Langley is waiting in the backseat of Cassie's car.

Just as soon as she turns the corner and is out of eye site, he pops up with the gun in his hand and demands, "You will drive me to the fairgrounds right now and no questions asked."

She jumps in her seat and screams with fright before she nearly runs off the road. Pulling over, she collects herself before yelling, "You almost gave me a heart attack. What is wrong with you?"

"I said take me there now!" he demands as he growls at her menacingly while thrusting the gun into her shoulder.

"Alright, already." She replies with her hands up and shaking.

She had no clue that her evening would begin like this or where it would end but for the moment all she had to do was to keep her cool, so she doesn't get her head blown clean off.

"Go!" he yells at the top of his lungs, as she practically jumps in her seat.

After realizing that if she doesn't drive him there, she may very well get shot, she quickly puts it back in gear and continues to their destination without asking.

"I just want to say I am sorry. I realize that this is not what you would have expected at the end of your shift but just know I am truly sorry for this." He states sadly before he raises the butt of his revolver and hits her hard over the back of the head.

Once she is hunched down in the front seat unconscious, he slides out and is careful to avoid detection by Deputy Carleson.

"Say, you haven't seen Sheriff Langley yet, have you?" the radio chirps as Sheriff Summerton's voice sounds loud and clear.

Deputy Carleson picks up his radio after finishing off the cup of coffee quickly and answers hesitantly, "No, why? Do you actually think he is stupid enough to come back out here?"

There is a silence on the radio before Sheriff Summerton replies, "Yes, I do. He seemed driven, even if he had to walk there."

"Alright. I have been here keeping an eye out. As soon as I see him, I will make sure he doesn't disturb anyone at the fairgrounds."

"Sounds good. Say, I am about to head out for the night. Do you want me to come by and relieve you in about an hour?" Sheriff Summerton asks thoughtfully as he puts all his papers away for the evening.

"No, it should be fine. I will stay for a few hours. If there is no trouble, I will just go home. Besides, you have my number and if there is anything after I leave, you know where to find me."

What he doesn't know is that behind the gate, the demons are having the time of their lives. They have even taken off their human suits and are dancing around the bonfire while chanting in expectation of what's to come in the moonlight.

"Ah, everyone. Now that we are all here. I want to express my gratitude for all your hard work. Tonight is a special night. After all, we have three meals for your delight.

Several of the boys went to town earlier while you were all cleaning up and found two babies for baby back ribs and a sweet little freckle faced toddler for toddler tartare. I can guarantee that tonight will be the best meal we have had in quite a long time." the ringmaster shouts as his eyes protrude from their sockets and his freakishly long black arms point to the still screaming toddler on the spit, turning in the fire.

As for the babies and their baby back ribs, two demons are busily cutting them up while they are still alive so they can be grilled. This way the mix of fear and blood flavors the meat with a special sort of seasoning that only living morsels have. If you listen closely, the cracking and sawing of bone can barely be heard over their cries as the demons tear them into bite sized portions for their delight.

"Is it time? Is it time?" a dwarf-sized demon asks excitedly as it looks up at the ringmaster with big, black bulbous eyes.

"Not yet. But I do believe that they are done cutting up the babies for the baby back ribs. Now, if you are patient, I bet they will be done in a few minutes, and you can be first in line."

"Oh boy, oh boy. First in line you say?" it asks with a huge devilish grin on its face.

"Why, yes." The ringmaster replies as he points to the spit and the meat that is already almost done.

After a few more minutes, the ringmaster notices that the food looks done and yells, "Remove the spit, and let's eat. Everything looks done to me."

As they quickly take the spit out of the fire and slam the slab of meat on the table, he notices next to it a plate of toddler tartare chopped up and made from the toddlers' arms and legs. Then he looks over to where the baby back ribs are grilling and commands, "Someone fetch me the ribs, I do believe the little one asked first."

Once they are plated up and laid on the table, it grabs a few baby back ribs, a chunk of roasted toddler and a spoonful of tartare for good measure. Then the ringmaster takes a baby back rib and the toddlers' jellied eyeballs before he steps back and yells loudly, "Please, by all means help yourselves."

While the ringmaster stands back and watches them all take ribs and chunks of roasted toddler, he gobbles down his food quickly. Suddenly, a truly loud and disgusting burp erupts from his stomach. They all turn around with blood, guts and skin on their faces as they stare at him before the crowd begins to laugh uncontrollably. When no one expects it Sheriff Langley rushes towards the ringmaster after getting an eyeful of the most horrendous display imaginable.

"What are you?" He screams before pulling his gun and shooting the ringmaster point blank in the face.

When the bullet goes right through him and doesn't faze him the least, Sheriff Langley's mouth drops open and he stands completely still, unable to comprehend what he just saw.

"What?" he asks as he drops the gun, and it suddenly goes off again.

This time when it discharges, it shoots Sheriff Langley in the chest, and he falls to the ground.

"No." he cries out while clutching his chest.

The moment the ringmaster hears Deputy Carleson yelling from the gate, he looks down at Sheriff Langley with the most incredibly evil smile on his face. The first thing he notices afterwards is that there is far too much blood pouring out of that wound for Sheriff Langley to live. When he looks up at Deputy Carleson scaling the gate, he begins to laugh wholeheartedly because he looks like a cartoon character as he slips and falls on the ground.

"How stupid you look." He murmurs under his breath before he turns around to see one of the tents on fire and Sheriff Langley beside it.

"How in the hell?"

Chapter 14: The Fire

When all the other demons notice the fire, they immediately start to run towards the tents while not thinking of the consequences.

"Hurry. We have to grab our human suits before they are lost." One demon says, then another before they all start to run in different directions.

Eventually, they knock each other down like dominoes.

"Stop!" Deputy Carleson screams with his phone in his hand after he calls Sheriff Summerton for backup and the Fire Department to put out the flames.

Unfortunately, it is far too late because it becomes a raging fire that is growing out of control by the minute. Standing back helplessly, he watches as Sheriff Langley wobbles towards him. Deputy Carleson sees the blood oozing out of the gaping hole in his chest and finds himself wondering how he is still standing but then quickly turns his attention to the low over hanging trees that are going up like kindling all around the fairgrounds. If they don't get there soon, they may have a full-scale forest fire on their hands.

"Sheriff Langley, do you think you can grab that axe over there and bring it to me?" Deputy Carleson asks quickly when Sheriff Langley finally makes it to the locked gate. "I think I can break the lock with it." He adds as a spark of hope begins to fill him.

He nods without saying a word as Deputy Carleson sees his face turn white, but he still manages to get the axe and bring it to him before he faints.

"Hold on." Deputy Carleson murmurs under his breath as he keeps one eye on Sheriff Langley while making sure he is still breathing, then he swings the axe at the lock.

Sure enough, he breaks it, and it comes crashing down to the ground in a loud smacking sound. Afterwards, he throws the axe to the side before pulling the gate open and moving Sheriff Langley outside. Deputy Carleson watches his labored breathing once again to make sure he is still alive and when he is convinced that he is fine for the moment, he hurries inside right before the fire trucks pull up.

When Deputy Carleson hears Sheriff Summerton's voice, he rushes towards the sirens to flag them down and yells at the top of his lungs, "Over here. We need an ambulance now. Sheriff Langley has been shot and is unconscious.

In the meantime, the Fire Department pulls out their hoses as they try to control the blazing inferno.

"Are you alright?" Sheriff Summerton asks Deputy Carleson with concern in his voice as he scans him up and down.

"What exactly happened?" He asks as they walk back to his car and lean against the hood.

"All I know is that one minute I was sitting in the car drinking coffee. The next, I heard a gunshot and then another a second or two later. I rushed out of the car and up to the gate as fast as I could, but it was locked.

At first, I just stared when I saw Sheriff Langley on the ground, but then I saw him get up and light one of the tents on fire. The whole time this was happening, it was like a blur of clowns running around in circles and screaming something strange. I couldn't see them very well because they were towards the back of the fairground, but when the ringmaster saw me, I realized that they weren't really scared of the fire, and he didn't entirely look all that human either.

When I tried to scale the gate, the ringmaster began to laugh at me, but then suddenly he went into one of the tents as soon as he saw they were catching on fire. After that I watched as Sheriff Langley slowly walked towards me with a gunshot wound in his chest. I thought for sure he would never make it to the gate, but when he did, I had him give me an axe and that is when I managed to break the lock.

I pulled him outside and was just about to go in and see how I could help when you arrived." Deputy Carleson replies quickly as he watches everyone rush by with axes and hoses to fight the fire.

"So did Sheriff Langley shoot the ringmaster or himself?"

"I am not all that sure because I wasn't standing there when it happened. I was still in the car oblivious of the situation. I didn't even see how Sheriff Langley got inside." Deputy Carleson admits as he starts to crash from the adrenaline rush.

"Here, why don't you sit down in my car?" Sheriff Summerton asks while taking his arm and helping him to the car.

"You stay here. I am going to see what I can do." He states authoritatively before he shuts Deputy Carleson's door.

Once Sheriff Summerton walks inside, he has to skirt around several Trucks as they try to fight the fire.

"You really shouldn't be in here right now. It's dangerous and everything is collapsing." The Fire Chief explains as he rushes around with a hose.

"I need to check and see if anyone is still alive." Sheriff Summerton yells and then walks forward when the Chief nods.

Unfortunately, the farther he moves into the fairgrounds, he realizes that nothing could possibly be still alive. What is even worse is when he stumbles upon the remains of the bonfire, he sees the spit and human bones the size of a small toddler. There are even tiny bones scattered around in the ashes that look like ribs from a baby.

He becomes horrified when he begins to think that this is where the missing children went to.

"No, there were midgets here. It had to be one of them, not one of our missing children. Please, God please." Sheriff Summerton murmurs under his breath as tears threaten to fall from his eyes.

He falls to his knees and cradles his head because this is just too much for one days' time.

"Hey, you need to get out of here. See that tree up there? It is about to come down right where we are." One of the firemen says quickly as he forces Sheriff Summerton to move just in time.

As he walks out of the fairgrounds, he hears a loud boom and then looks back to see the remnants of a burning tree right where he was kneeling just a minute earlier.

Eventually, hours later they get the blaze under control, but they don't find the clowns, the ringmaster or any of the animals. They do however confirm that partially torn apart bodies of a toddler and two babies were found in the wreckage fairground as they combed the smoldering ashes for answers.

Chapter 15: Afterwards

"How are you feeling this morning?" Deputy Carleson asks Sheriff Langley as he sits up in bed at Saint Mary Memorial Hospital.

"To tell you the truth, I have been better. The exercises they are having me do are ridiculous and just make my chest hurt worse. They are supposed to make me better not try to kill me." he says sarcastically as a young nurse in her 20s walks in with needles to take blood.

"Oh, good. The vampires are here to take my blood again." Sheriff Langley adds grouchier than ever as he shrinks down in his bed and rolls his eyes.

"Well, I will leave you to it then. I just wanted to let you know that there was no trace of them at the fairgrounds. So, take that as you will but I am hoping they never return to Coupeville if they did get out alive." Deputy Carleson says briefly before leaning down and whispering into Sheriff Langley's ear, "I don't know if this was a figment of my imagination or not, but I could have sworn that at least the ringmaster was not human. Did you see that too?"

Sheriff Langley nods slowly before the nurse pokes him in the left arm and he winces.

"Thank you for that." Deputy Carleson says softly before he walks out the door.

Upon returning to his car, he sits down and closes his eyes before recalling the events of the night before.

"What were they then?" he asks himself before he hears an all too familiar song being carried by the wind.

He quickly opens his eyes to scan the parking lot but sees nothing at first. However, when he turns the car on a few minutes later, a red balloon flies across the hood and the song returns louder this time. As he puts it in reverse and looks in the rearview mirror he jumps because he sees a brief image of the ringmaster smiling eerily at him with bulging eyeballs that are hanging from their eye sockets.

"Was it real?" he asks himself moments later as he looks around and the ringmaster is gone.

"Or was it a figment of his imagination?"

Years later when Deputy Carleson becomes Sheriff Carleson, he hears a tale of a circus that comes once in late October and with-it disappearances of small children.

If you were him, would you go after them, or choose to dismiss the tale as merely a good horror story?

The End

I hope you enjoyed The Circus Is Back. Please review it after reading and then look for my other books.

About the Author

M.D. LaBelle is an international award-winning, bestselling multi genre author. Her genres include horror, dark romance, fantasy, thriller, romance, psychological thriller, youth horror, and children's books. They can be found on all major online bookstores, plus some indie bookstores, as well as a few physical ones. She lives in Mount Pleasant, Michigan with her loving husband and 4 of her children. While she spends most of her time writing, she also has a degree in Art from Central Michigan University and is a violinist. After following her on social media, please check out her books on any of the bookstores and at her website/bookstore at https://www.mdlabelle.com

www.instagram.com/M.D.LaBelle/

Twitter Account

www.twitter.com/MDLaBelle1

Facebook Account

www.facebook.com/profile.php?id=100062142582314

I hope you enjoyed reading The Circus Is Back. Please take the time to read all my other novels if you haven't already. Thank you.

Review it. Please review this novel and let others know what you liked about this book. If you want, please visit me at
www.mdlabelle.com

The Circus Is Back

Paperback Edition

Copyright © 2024 M.D. LaBelle

Casper Publishing

All Rights Reserved

This book is a work of fiction. Characters and names are of the author's imagination or are used fictitiously. Any resemblance to an actual person, living or dead, is entirely coincidental.

All rights are reserved. No part of this publication may be reproduced, distributed, or transmitted in any form or by any means, including photocopying, recording, or other electronic or mechanical methods, without the express prior written permission of the publisher, except in the case of brief quotations embodied in critical reviews and certain other noncommercial uses permitted by copyright law. For permission requests, please contact the author through her website: www.mdlabelle.com

www.ingramcontent.com/pod-product-compliance
Lightning Source LLC
LaVergne TN
LVHW061624070526
838199LV00070B/6570